MIJ KELLY AND ROSS COLLINS

WHERE GIANTS HIDE

sourcebooks
jabberwocky

I went hunting for giants.
I searched far and wide.
They're bigger than houses.

So **where** do they hide?

Where

is

the

fairy

who'll

grant

me

a

wish?

And **what happened** to mermaids?

Did they **turn** into fish?

they **don't** turn into princes.

If I try riding **broomsticks,** they **won't** budge two inches.

So don't say there's a **troll** lurking under the bridge.

Don't tell me that goblins are raiding my fridge.

Or that magic is knocking **tip-tap** at my door...

because I don't **believe** it exists any more.

If it did, we'd have **pixies** to keep the house clean,

terrible
dragons

to make us all

scream,

and strange, **see-through genies**
like great puffs of steam.

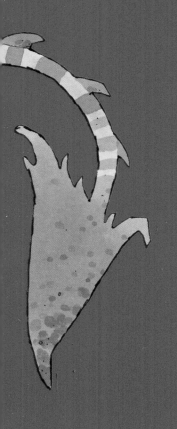

But these things aren't **real.**

The world's dull and grey
and if there ever was **magic,**
it's

all

leaked

away...

And
that
makes
me
sad.

How **I wish** that, right now,
the world would stand up
and take a **big bow**,

and do something

amazing...

...to make me go "WOW!"

Something amazing, especially for me.
And that's when I wonder, hey,
what would it be?

And that's when I see
I can dream it alive,
and that's when I know...

Oh! That's where giants hide!

To Ralph - M.K.

For Nick, Sam, Ruby and Finlay - R.C.

by Mij Kelly

and Ross Collins

Published by Sourcebooks Jabberwocky, an imprint of Sourcebooks, Inc.
P.O. Box 4410, Naperville, Illinois 60567-4410
(630) 961-3900
Fax: (630) 961-2168
www.jabberwockykids.com

First published in 2009 by Hodder Children's Books, a division of Hachette Children's Books.

Library of Congress Cataloging-in-Publication data is on file with the publisher.

Source of Production: Wing King Tong Co. Ltd., Hong Kong
Date of Production: 12/2009
Run Number: 11324

Printed and bound in China
WKT 10 9 8 7 6 5 4 3 2 1